OUTRIDERS

BY

Guy Cain

Guy Cain

Outriders is dedicated to all the people who have been misclassified by the powers that be. The artists forced by circumstances to be warriors. The ones with troubled spirits who smile to calm the storm in others. The ones for whom the battle seems unending.

Special thanks to Art Friedl for the amazing cover. I truly appreciate all your help.

CHAPTER ONE – EARTH

Earth has been a shithole for decades. Over farming, overfishing, over mining. Anything mankind could do, it did to excess. Switching to a World Government helped for a while by allowing the free movement of resources, but it wasn't enough. Our planet was rapidly becoming a barren wasteland. All the resources we could scrounge were allocated to looking for new planets to exploit. Anyplace with resources the Earth could use to its benefit. Finally, they found a planet with an atmosphere that would sustain human life. Then another and another. Each new planet was colonized and industrialized as quickly as possible. Each became a steppingstone to the next. Mankind, it seemed, was alone in the universe and free to pillage at will.

As you might imagine, most people wanted to get off the Earth. Go to one of the more hospitable and beautiful planets where the air was clean, the water clear, and the living easy. The powers that be set up a screening process. The best and the brightest were given first choice. The population of each colonized planet was limited to avoid making the same mistakes as on Earth. Ultimately each planet would have to produce something of value. Something it could send back to Earth as a sort of tax. Raw materials, foods, anything that would benefit the people. Well, the people who mattered anyway.

To be clear, the people who benefit are not the people you see on the streets. Definitely not anyone you're likely to run into on a daily basis. You see it's nearly impossible for an average man to survive on Earth. I started working in the landfill mines when I was twelve. Five years later I could afford a three hundred square foot apartment, only because I split the rent with a prostitute who worked in the area. Even then there were days when I didn't have enough credits for food. That's the main reason I decided to join the Colonial Security Forces. Not only would they get me off Earth, they would keep me fed, and they paid better than the mines.

The preliminary testing for the CSF was invasive to say the least. From each candidate bodily fluids were extracted. Not just blood, but every type of bodily fluid, including some I didn't even know I had. They also took hair, skin and stool samples. Throughout the process, we were treated like cattle. They even went so far as to assign us numbers, which were then written on our upper arm, across our chest and on our back. When they were finished, we were told to get dressed and leave. Three days later I received a notification saying I had passed. The notification had my name followed by the number I had been assigned during screening.

Twenty-four hours later I was on a transport to the Colonial Security Forces Space Station for Receiving and Classification. Immediately upon arrival we were issued plain white clothing. One size fits all shirts and drawstring pants. The numbers they had assigned us on Earth were quickly stenciled onto our new clothes. For five days they checked our intelligence, psychiatric stamina, genetic makeup, the whole battery. The doctors and nurses wouldn't even look the recruits in the eye. We were just specimens to them. They would explain the procedure, conduct it, then point us to the next one. At the end of each day's tests, recruits were sent back to the barracks where they must remain until being escorted to the dining hall.

Approximately sixty five percent of all recruits simply didn't pass due to psychological issues and were sent back to Earth. Those of us who were deemed "suitable" by the medical personnel were placed in semi-private quarters to await our assignment and travel orders. It was obviously an efficient system. Later, I would come to realize that it was the only efficient system in the entire Colonial Security Forces.

After only two days I received my orders. I had been assigned to Indigo Divum and would be leaving in a few weeks. The doctors gave me several shots and I had orders to return every other day for an additional "treatment." The remainder of my time on the station was to be spent lifting weights or running on a treadmill. Later I would discover that the shots were steroids to help build muscle mass. The voyage to Indigo Divum is approximately thirty months, passengers would be in stasis for most of the trip. In stasis, the body tends to atrophy, so they wanted us to bulk up as much as possible before we left the space station.

CHAPTER TWO - INDIGO DIVUM

The shuttle ride down to the surface was amazing. Indigo Divum is a beautiful planet, when seen from the air. Approximately twenty percent of it is covered in gorgeous blue water. The land is mostly desert and looks like gold when seen from high above with thin green ribbons of vegetation surrounding all the crater-shaped lakes. When you step off the shuttle the first thing you notice is how good the air feels in your lungs. I thought it was a side effect of being in stasis or maybe spending my life on the polluted Earth. Turns out that Indigo Divum has an oxygen content of thirty six percent. That's about one and a half times the oxygen our bodies are accustomed to on Earth.

Colonial Security Forces set up training camps on every planet the Earth has claimed. The idea is to train the foreign recruits in the atmosphere they will be working to get them climatized. On the planets with larger populations, CSF will draw from the general population, saving the trouble of transporting people all the way from Earth. Indigo Divum doesn't have anywhere near the populace for that so most of us came from Earth with a few coming from other colonies. After a couple months the training was complete, and we were assigned to our units. Two days before I was to go to a warehouse security detail I got into a scrape with an officer.

I slugged a lieutenant for trying to convince a recruit to be a bit friendlier with him. She didn't feel like doing it, but he was stronger than her. Anyway, the LT wanted me dead. The Captain was more than willing to put me in front of the firing squad even with the recruits sworn statement. In the end, it was simple mathematics. Every man we could field was an asset, even "undesirables," so the Colonel made me an outrider.

Nobody thought I'd last more than six months. That was nearly five years ago.

CHAPTER THREE - OUTRIDERS

Getting assigned as an Outrider was supposed to be a death sentence. It still is for some, I guess, but it's typically their own choice. We were getting a bit of a reputation as being tougher than the average soldier. Rumor has it that there have been a few official requests to join. Seems unlikely even with all the changes over the last couple years, but maybe it's true.

When I got to the Outriders Platoon, we totaled sixteen men. There was no platoon leader, as he had not come back from the previous patrol. Besides, sixteen is hardly enough to necessitate anything more than a sergeant. In time, I learned that no lieutenant wanted to join the OrP and no commissioned officer was willing to promote a miscreant from within our ranks. They showed me the ropes while we were on base, got me equipped and gave me a run-down of our duties. Three days later we left the base.

We were assigned to a small company that was moving north to reinforce a new base. Our job was to "serve as forward observers, flank guards, and make first contact when necessary in order to give the company time to assume a defensive posture." It all sounds very official, but the truth is, we were assigned to absorb enemy fire, nothing more.

Looking at the map, I guessed it to be a full four-day trip, possibly five if any of the vehicles had mechanical issues, or some moron lieutenant got us lost. Either one seemed likely and it wasn't outside the realm of possibility for both to happen.

The first day was easy enough. OrP ran forward and flank patrols as usual, but we all knew nothing was going to happen that close to the main base where reinforcements were readily available. Sarge said late second day or early on the third would be when we were most vulnerable. He was right.

Early on the third day, just as the convoy cleared some dunes, they hit the column. Rising out of the sand, weapons set to single fire they made the first volley count taking out two or three of ours for every one of theirs. Some green LT was screaming over the radio that the marauders were nearly in our ranks and that OrP should return to catch them in a crossfire. Sarge stomped that shit quick, telling us to keep to our patrol and watch for vehicles.

No sooner had he given the order then we saw them. There were only three deuce-tracks but each one bristled with men and guns. Marauders hung onto every part of the vehicles, running boards, hoods, anyplace they could hold on. They fired wildly as they approached the column. Sarge came on the radio again telling us to flank the tracks and "herd them towards the convoy." Easy enough as they were dead set on going that way. We started firing from the sides and rear, the main column opened with the big blasters and within seconds the tracks were exploding sending flaming body parts in every direction.

The encounter had lasted only four minutes but that was long enough. It was tough to get an accurate body count. Many of the rauders had been literally cut to pieces by the one-inch blasters mounted on our big J-tracks. OrP didn't have anything bigger than .30 cal blasters on our speed-tracks but we got the job done. Furthermore, we had saved the day without losing a single man. Sarge was very pleased with our performance.

Once everything got settled and the convoy was ready to move, that green LT came over to shout at Sarge for disobeying orders. He got out maybe a dozen words when the old man put out a cigarette on the lieutenant's crisp uniform. The LT drew back a fist and then froze as three .30 cal blasters were turned slightly in his direction. That's when the old man explained the reality of it all. OrP had done the right thing by sticking to their position, hemming in the rauder's tracks. If we had obeyed the LT's orders OrP would have been caught between the convoy's one inchers and the marauders guns. Most likely the entire convoy would have been lost. Begrudgingly, the LT gave our sergeant a nod and walked away.

We arrived at Gold Base Twelve without further incident. Most of the tracks and gear were being permanently assigned to GB12, with only a few returning empty along the same route we had taken to get there. The rauders probably wouldn't bother attacking the empty tracks, but we still had to guard them as we would be repeating the drill when the next base needed to be resupplied. That gave us about a week at GB12 while the officers checked inventory and filed the necessary paper-work.

As long as we were there, the commander figured he'd put us to work running patrols around the base. Our sergeant came up with a "supplementary plan." The first day all sixteen of us went out on speed-tracks, two men to an ST, a driver and a gunner as usual. We started one click from base and slowly spiraled out to about seven clicks making note of any landscape a solitary man could use for concealment. Just after dusk we returned to base and found Sarge with a big topo-map. After a couple hours of discussion, we chose five separate locations, all on different rock formations that had a good field of view. The next day we put the plan into action.

At sun-up five patrols went out on speed-tracks manned only by a driver. Periodically one would stop at a rock formation to relieve himself or have a smoke. There's a small storage area behind the seats of a speed-track, just big enough to hide a man. When the driver stopped, the hidden man would carefully slither out and secrete himself amongst the rocks. At dusk the driver made a final stop and left a pack of gear. As soon as the sun was down the hidden Outrider would grab the pack and set up his listening post.

The job of a listening post is to stay awake all night and watch for enemy movement. To that purpose each LP had a small thermal imaging screen, a radio to contact sarge if needed, water ration, a stimtab to keep him alert, one Hex-MPED, one P-15 MPED (manually propelled explosive device), and a side arm. There had been quite a bit of discussion concerning the pistol. Nobody wanted to be out there alone without a longarm. Sarge ended the argument when he explained that the LP was strictly forbidden from engaging the enemy. Their job was to observe and report enemy movement, use the MPEDs to get the attention of the base guards in the event of an impending attack. The handgun was simply a precaution to prevent being taken captive.

Things were quiet the first couple nights. No movement reported. As the sun came up, we sent out the morning patrols. They stopped at the rocks like before, but this time the Outrider who had spent the night slipped back into the little cargo area. One at a time the patrols would return to the base under the guise of refueling. While inside, the driver would pick up a new Outrider to man the LP for the coming night, then drop him off like before. The whole system worked well and while it was not a pleasant feeling to be out there alone all night, it was still better than unloading trucks under the watchful gaze of the base officers.

***

Marauders are a strange people. They live the life of a nomad out there in the desert, scraping out an existence by preying on anyone they happen to cross paths with, even other bands of marauders were fair game. The only loyalty they have is to the leader of their particular group. Occasionally we hear reports of some great holy man or warrior who is uniting all the desert tribes with designs to take on the rest of the world. Rarely does the union last longer than a season before someone is caught with some other man's wife or daughter and all hell breaks loose. Intelligence Division has yet to provide any reliable information on just how many of them are out there, with estimates ranging from one to ten thousand scattered across the sands.

The origins of the marauders seems to be lost in legend, but they obviously came here as colonists. For one reason or another they were not able to get along with the others and set out on their own. Early records indicate some people were even banished to the desert by their fellow colonists for committing some crime or another. No matter how you look at it, or what you choose to believe, they are an uncivilized bunch of killers.

For us, the real trouble comes when the enemy befriends them. The group that attacked us on the way out had probably been encouraged and supplied by our enemies, the Indingos. They'll use marauders to harass us every chance they get.

Sometimes they even use them to bolster their forces for an attack on one of our settlements. It's a tenuous union at best and it typically only lasts through a single battle. Afterwards the rauders plunder and steal from both ally and foe alike before disappearing back into the desert.

****

Somewhere around 0200 on the fifth night one of our LPs picked up movement with the infrared. The Outrider radioed sarge to report movement approximately two clicks out. He counted six men moving slowly towards his position. Soon after all the LPs were reporting similar movement. Sarge ordered them to turn off their equipment, maintain radio silence and stay out of sight. With a little luck, the rauders would walk right past the LP without taking notice. Inside GB12 our unit got ready for an attack.

The next four hours we waited for the sun to come up or the shooting to start. When the sun finally broke the horizon there was still no activity outside the base. Sarge thought maybe it was just a bunch of marauders trying to get a better look at the layout. No matter what or who, we decided to get our men out of those rocks as usual, but we'd wait until late afternoon to re-man the listening posts.

It was my turn to drive an ST. As I was doing a pre-patrol inspection it occurred to me that our speed-tracks were probably the most valuable piece of equipment the OrP had. These things would run on sand, through mud, over rocks, even snow not that there was any snow on this planet, and they used very little fuel. The thirty-caliber blaster mounted to the front could be operated by the driver if needed or better yet by a gunner riding in the passenger seat. That's when it all came together for me.

As the first ST started to pull out of the motor-pool I yelled for him to stop before waving in the other drivers. On our way here, we had seen the marauders bury themselves in the sand then rise up to ambush the column. The LPs had reported just over thirty men total. Even three times that number couldn't take on the entire base. They weren't planning to attack the base; they were planning to ambush the patrols. Four consecutive days we had been stopping at those same rocks at least twice a day. Six marauders would be more than enough to take out a solo Outrider in his speed-track. We quickly came up with a plan and ran it by Sarge before grabbing our gunners.

Rather than circling out then heading for the rocks as before, each speed-track made a straight line for the LP he had been assigned, making an effort to approach from the side closest to the base. Our hope was that the marauders, if they were still there, would be on the far side of the rock formations. My ST was assigned to pick up LP3, as we got close, our man could be seen crouching in the rocks, intently scrutinizing the desert beyond. We slowed to an idle just short of the rocks as he rose to throw one then a second MPED into the midst of the cloaked figures materializing not twenty meters away. The P-15 went off first, sending a white-hot spray of burning metal in every direction. My gunner opened with the thirty just as the smoke from the hex-MPED was starting to spread out. Our man sprinted to the ST and dove behind the seats. I threw the speed-track in reverse and began to back quickly away, allowing the gunner to keep firing towards the rauders, even if we couldn't see them through the smoke.

All around the base this same scene was playing out. We headed towards LP2 and fired into the smoke as the ST was backing away just as we had. A quick radio check confirmed that all five LPs had been picked up successfully and were on the way back to the relative safety of the base.

Inside the base it was pandemonium as soldiers scrambled to ready themselves for an enemy onslaught. A lieutenant met us at the gate insisting that we report to the commander at once. As we approached the commander's office, the only solid structure on base, the door opened and Sarge stepped out with a big smile on his face. The official story he gave the CO was something along the lines of "OrP forces, while on standard patrol, encountered a sizable enemy force and repelled same without loss of personnel or equipment." We were now "two for two" and feeling damn good about it.

CHAPTER FOUR -
SUCK A BIG ONE

The base we are assigned to work from is officially named Supply Base 01. The Colonial Security Forces is not known for being creative. It was the first base established on Indigo Divum and is by far the largest on the planet. It is also the first one that new recruits see when they arrive since it has the planet's only landing area for shuttles and the planet's only training facility. The enlisted men stationed here have come up with their own name for SB01, typically referring to it as "Suck a Big One."

Suck a Big One is also the largest city on Indigo Divum. It consists of row upon row of metal buildings. All of them are the same dimension and color. Some are barracks, others are warehouses, commissary, dining halls, hospitals, hydroponic gardens, you name it. Because they all look alike, every building has a sign with large block letters denoting the exact purpose of that building. Ours reads "Outrider Platoon Barracks+Motor Pool." Because there are so few of us, half of our barracks was turned into a maintenance area for our speedtracks. The only real problem with that is that we have never been given a mechanic. With our recent victory at Gold Base Twelve, sarge figured he could get one assigned to us permanently.

Unfortunately, according Colonial Security Force policy, "the unit must have at least twelve small, six mid-size, three large motor vehicles, or some combination of the aforementioned to warrant a maintenance technician assignment." Technically speaking we had ten speed-tracks, although two of them appeared to be beyond repair and were currently resting under a tarp in our barracks/garage. The obvious solution was to requisition two more speed-tracks giving OrP a total of twelve small vehicles.

The problem was, as the quartermaster informed sarge, with only sixteen men in our unit we were already "over equipped" with the ten speed-tracks we currently had. Sarge was about to go light speed and shouted, "I'm not asking for a damn deuce! Just two fucking speed-tracks!"

The quartermaster was slightly shaken by the outburst but stuck to the regs. "Your unit is entitled to a deuce for the purposes of carrying additional gear and supplies as needed, but you are not getting any additional speed-tracks!"

And that is how we ended up with a deuce-track and a mechanic of our own.

The mechanic was new to Indigo Divum. He had just completed training and was not excited about being assigned to the OrP. It seems our reputation for being troublemakers was well known throughout Supply Base 01, but it didn't take him long to realize he had an easy gig. Just keep our speed-tracks running and nobody was going to bother him. Anyone who tried to interfere with his job would have to go through the sarge first.

It took our new mechanic nearly three weeks to get all eight STs up to spec. None of us knew enough to adjust the tracks as the belts stretched, or to lube the suspension and bearings. Most of us had no idea what those little grease nipples were. After he was satisfied, they were all in field worthy condition, he spoke with sarge and the two of them organized a "field maintenance class" for us. We had been doing our pre-patrol inspections, but these machines were the backbone of the OrP and it just made sense that we know some basics about how to fix them. The last thing any of us wanted was to be stranded out there in the sand. Especially if it was something simple that could be rigged up long enough for us to limp back. Ultimately, this knowledge would save several lives.

In the months since joining the Outriders I had noticed some changes. Our platoon was working together as a unit more so now than before. While I couldn't be certain, it felt to me like sarge was the one responsible. I asked some of the others about the lieutenant they had before I came on. Apparently, he was trying to make a name for himself, hoping to get out of the OrP. The LT wouldn't accept input from any of the men, especially sarge. He was more concerned about uniform and barracks inspections than he was about marauder tactics. On the day he disappeared, rumor has it he went out on a speed-track by himself, hoping to catch one of our patrols goofing off. His last check in was about six clicks from SB01. They searched for him, but couldn't find any trace of him or his ST. Since then sarge had been handling things.

***

For the next few months we did nothing more than run patrols around SB01. One-man patrols were acceptable out to three clicks. Anything beyond that and we were required to carry a gunner. I enjoyed the close patrols most, since it gave me some time alone to relax and enjoy the beauty of Indigo Divum. Suck a Big One was located on the edge of the green belt surrounding a very large lake. You could just barely make out the opposite shore with your naked eye. The water was beautiful. It appeared to be dark blue, almost black, when I'd seen it from the shuttle. Up close it was clear as glass. You could drop a rock in near the shore where it quickly became deep and watch it fall the twenty feet to the bottom. During training we were warned repeatedly about staying out of the water. They claimed during the early colonization quite a few people had been lost to the things that live in it. Even the Marauders won't cross the water. Come to think of it, I've never even heard of any boats on this planet. Dangerous as it may be, it is beautiful. Far more beautiful than anything you will ever see on Earth.

The plant life here is different too. The plants

that grow at the water's edge are a dark green. As you move away from the water, they become lighter, finally ending up almost white where they intrude on the sand. No doubt some scientist could explain the logic behind it all, but I'm just an Outrider who occasionally sneaks away to enjoy some solitude.

Word came down the Engineers would soon be off to lay the groundwork for a new base. Once established, this one was set to be a mining operation with a large civilian population. As expected, we would be escorting the column of heavy equipment. Most likely we would be away from SB01 for months. With that in mind, sarge decided we should load the newly acquired deuce with all the spare parts we could get our hands on, including one of the busted speed-tracks and our new mechanic. Once we reached the location, we could set up a maintenance area and rotate our speed-tracks out as needed. Not to mention, with a deuce there would be plenty of room to carry "personal items" like alcohol, tobacco, and other necessities. With that in mind, we were almost looking forward to the mission.

For the next two weeks Engineers loaded heavy equipment onto flatbed trailers. Once a trailer was full and the equipment properly chained down it was moved to a staging area just outside the gates. To the Engineers this seemed like a wonderful idea as it would be an easy process for the column to form up and move out. Those of us who were charged with protecting the column knew better. By the time we finally left SB01 every marauder on ID would know about it.

The good news was nearly a hundred CSF regulars would be part of the procession. That meant four or five J-tracks mounted with one-inch blasters. Maybe a few half-inchers mounted to their personnel carriers too. According to sarge the Engineers were not great marksmen, but they could be counted on to "spray and pray" if the column came under fire. All things considered, there would be plenty of firepower on this trip.

CHAPTER FIVE - MOE16

When the day came for the column to move out, there were five fuel tankers, four flatbeds of heavy equipment, four flatbeds of building materials, six personnel carriers, four J-tracks, thirteen deuce-tracks including ours, four half-tracks for officers, and our eight speed-tracks. Rumors were flying about it being the largest column ever to leave SB01. Whether the rumors were true or not, it made for one hell of a big target.

No sooner had the rear of the column lost sight of Suck a Big One than the sun started to set. The officers decided it would be best to keep moving through the night since the men were well rested and we could easily call for support from the base if needed. It wasn't a terrible decision, unless you were an Outrider. Traveling all night meant we had to stay out in the speed-tracks all night. Sarge gave us the nod to use stimtabs if needed as we would ultimately be on duty forty hours straight. As the morning dawned my gunner offered to drive so I could "rest my eyes." It was nearly impossible to sleep in the hard-composite seats of a speed-track, but I gave it a try anyway.

Around mid-day sarge called in one ST at a time so we could sit in the back of the deuce and eat.

We had thirty minutes to relax before we went back out and the next ST came in. It wasn't much, but it sure helped. They halted the column just after dusk on the second day. We stayed out until it was fully dark then returned to the deuce for a quick meeting.

Sarge brought us current on everything he had heard. The column was scheduled to be at the mining location on day eight. Starting tomorrow one of the officers would be taking a half-track out for reconnaissance each morning. They had asked for a speed-track to accompany them. Sarge had suggested that two speed-tracks go and to his surprise they had agreed. The half-track would take point with the STs flanking. Sarge would ride in one of the gunner seats on these forays to act as a buffer between the officer and the Outriders. None of us had any objections to this.

The morning of day six, the reconnaissance team returned early having sighted marauders moving to the north. It was a large group and they seemed to be moving slowly and carrying far too much to be planning a raid. The column was in no danger of crossing paths with them and sarge believed they were simply moving their camp. After all, that's what nomads do. Still it was possible they had been watching us and were planning to set up an ambush along our current trajectory. In the end the column changed course slightly, just to be safe. According to the maps, the following afternoon our new course would bring us close to one of the smaller lakes that dotted Indigo Divum.

Around midday on day seven we could see the greenbelt surrounding the lake. The usual recon team went ahead to check the location. When they returned the officers decided we should set up camp at the lake. It would give us a couple hours of daylight to go through the vehicles and correct any issues rather than breaking down and holding up the entire column. Also, with the lake on one side we could more easily defend our position. The course change and early stop was going to cost us nearly a full day, but most agreed it was the best decision.

At the lake, the column set up camp with the CSF regulars creating a perimeter. The OrP made patrols around the camp using five of our speed tracks while the mechanic and remaining Outriders performed the necessary maintenance on the others. Once a speed-track had been fixed to the mechanic's satisfaction it went out to replace one on patrol. We kept rotating like that until all the STs were back to spec.

I had just pulled my speed-track in and shut her down when we heard men yelling near the lake. With the regulars on the perimeter, we grabbed our longarms and ran towards the commotion. Several of the engineers, having nothing better to do, had gathered at the edge of the lake to relax. One of the men claimed he could swim further and faster than anyone there. A second man took up the challenge and the rest made bets. Both men stripped down to their boxers and stood at the edge waiting for the signal. Somebody yelled "go" and both men dove in simultaneously. When neither man resurfaced the engineers on shore had begun yelling. The water was still and clear as it always was, yet there was no sign of the two swimmers. They had simply disappeared. The engineers were confined to their specific vehicles for the remainder of our stay at the lake. Nobody talked about it or went near the water afterwards.

The captain in charge of this venture was not happy about losing the Engineers. The resulting fury made for a very early departure the following morning. In his eyes he was now a day behind and two men short. All of us in the OrP could see where this was going. We went about our duties and waited to hear from sarge. Sure enough, just before noon, sarge contacted us by radio to pass along the captain's orders. The column would once again be driving through the night.

To soften the blow, sarge decided to relieve each team for one hour. We'd come in and meet him at the deuce, he would take our speed-track back out and run solo. It doesn't sound like much, but I can tell you not one of us complained. And believe it or not, it was surprisingly easy to fall asleep on the floor of that deuce-track as it made its way over the sands. Much later that evening sarge radioed the patrols, "Coffee's on me tonight." That was the wink and nudge we had all been waiting for. It seemed that even over the roar of motors you could hear stimtabs being opened and swallowed whole.

Sometime around noon on the ninth day, we arrived at the future home of Mining Operations Emplacement Sixteen. It looked like nothing more than a black rock shelf elevated a few feet above the sand. The engineers unrolled meter square papers and set up holo-projectors with satellite link antennae hooked to them. The CSF boys did their best to set up a defensive perimeter but had a tough time since MOE16 was nothing more than a bunch of trucks trying to figure out where to park. The OrP had it a little easier. Our job, as always, was to simply circle around the overpriced equipment, "and make first contact when necessary in order to give the company time to assume a defensive posture."

By the time the sun went down, Engineers, officers, and truck drivers were getting into a rhythm. There was some discussion about using the lights from the vehicles, so they could work until morning, but in the end the idea was discarded. The CSF regulars would have to stay up half the night as it was, and they were already nearing the point of exhaustion. Sarge volunteered our platoon to assist with guard duties, but the Captain declined the offer allowing us to get some much-needed rest. Afterall, stimtabs can only take you so far.

The next morning only four of the speedtracks went out on patrol. Sarge ordered the remaining four to stay behind for "maintenance purposes." The men relaxed in the shade of the deuce until mealtime then went out to relieve the ones on patrol. Sarge felt we had earned a little extra time off and who were we to argue with him. Besides, he had a plan to set up listening posts as we had done at Gold Base Twelve and he wanted us well rested.

By the end of day three, MOE16 was bustling with heavy equipment. Dozers and graders leveled the area around the rock shelf while heavy lifters unloaded the building materials and mining equipment. Six-meter-long metal poles were being driven into the sand at regular intervals by a machine designed specifically for the job. Following behind in an uncovered deuce, men threw off rolls of fencing that when attached to the poles would form the base perimeter. The whole thing looked like a well-orchestrated ballet of man and machine.

Meanwhile, OrP were out in force looking for places to set up listening posts. There was no doubt in our minds that all this activity would draw the attention of any marauders who might be in the area. The problem came when we failed to find any suitable locations. The only rock formation for ten clicks was the one we were currently building on. We all agreed the LPs would be an important part of the base defenses, at least until the CSF got everything fortified.

With no immediate cover we were at a loss as to how to hide the LPs. One of the Outriders who had been on an LP at Gold Base Twelve when it was attacked finally spoke up. He had seen the marauders rise out of the sand that morning. Apparently, they had not been buried per se but were simply covered in sand colored cloaks. They would stand up, toss the blanket or cloak to the side and begin shooting. Sarge was nodding as the Outrider related what he had seen. When the man finished sarge spoke up.

"It's just camouflage. CSF discarded the idea years ago when they realized that no one type worked on every planet. Hell, we can do it ourselves. We'll need at least two of the canvas covers off a deuce. See if you can find some laying unattended then meet back here in a couple hours."

The covers were easy to find. Typically, they were removed to facilitate unloading, rolled up and left next to the deuce. With everyone being busy it was a simple matter for two of us to pick up the roll from the ends and carry it away.

I still had doubts about the plan, especially since the covers were white, nowhere near the color of the golden metallic sands on Indigo Divum. But sarge had a solution for that too. We laid the covers out and cut each one in half resulting in four large squares of white canvas. Then our mechanic produced a couple gallons of oil from a drum and poured it onto the squares. It spread out and slowly soaked in turning the canvas a bit yellow. Sarge began shoveling handfuls of sand onto the canvas. Once they were covered, he lifted each one by the edge and shook off the excess leaving a fine grit sticking to the oily canvas. It was a nearly perfect match.

***

From the moment a recruit set foot on Indigo Divum there were Instructors telling him what to do. Where to stand. How to stand. Where to go. When to eat. Sixteen hours a day for the first thirty days of training the recruit had no time to think. We just did whatever we were told. Somewhere around the halfway point they started letting up. We would get a couple hours in the evening with no supervision. Most of the recruits would gamble or tell stories about what they had been through back home. I'm not much of a gambler and chose to spend my time researching the planet.

Indigo Divum was colonized nearly a half a century ago. The atmosphere is like Earth's, but with higher levels of oxygen. Only about twenty percent of the planet is covered in water and that is spread out in crater pockets across the surface. The first colonists found very little animal life on the planet. Many claimed to have seen birdlike creatures in small flocks, but nobody ever successfully caught one and after a few years no more sighting were reported.

In order to become self-sufficient, colonists had to establish agriculture. However, all attempts at large scale farming failed. The soil near the large bodies of water should have supported several standard Earth crops, but according to the reports, most died of "chlorosis" or "nitrogen deficiency" prior to harvest resulting in an average ten percent yield. Irrigation of the sandy soil was unsuccessful as well. Most colonists resorted to small gardens in the very center of the green belts that surrounded the lakes in order to produce a limited variety of fruits and vegetables.

Indigo Divum doesn't really have four seasons like Earth. Instead the four hundred and twenty-three-day year is broken in to only two seasons based on whether the amount of daylight is increasing or decreasing. The weather is consistently in the 20-30 degree Celsius range during the summer. Winter weather drops to a blustery 10-15 degrees. Rainfall is listed as "zero" on the official register for every year recorded since colonization began.

While the initial colonization had clearly not gone as planned, Earth continued to send people and resources to the planet. Ultimately children would be born here and that is where the real trouble began. As they grew these children considered themselves to be the indigenous peoples of Indigo Divum and called themselves Indingos. As adults they separated themselves from the colonists, insisting that those not born on Indigo Divum had no right to be here.

As the colonists were not only unwilling, but truly unable to pack up and leave, the Indingos revolted. Blood was shed and fearing reprisal from Earth, the Indingos fled. They went to the nearest greenbelt and set up their own small community. It would take nearly two years for word of the revolution to reach Earth and nearly another year for Colonial Security Forces to arrive. During that time the Indingos pillaged the other settlements at will, taking food, farming equipment, anything they felt might be of use to them.

When the first CSF unit arrived, they immediately went to the Indingos' community only to find it deserted. For days they searched, spreading out across the sands in an attempt to find and bring the Indingos to justice. Nobody knows for certain what happened to those units, but none of the CSF servicemen ever returned.

Several additional CSF units had been dispatched to Indigo Divum and they began arriving only days after the disappearance of the first. These units were tasked with defending the remaining colonists. They put up fencing, gates, towers, and metal buildings to keep the colonists safe. CSF shuttles continued to arrive, bringing more soldiers, supplies, and even more colonists. Eventually the settlement would grow into Supply Base 01.

***

Mining Operations Emplacement 16 was coming together quickly. Three metal buildings were completely assembled and much of the mining equipment had already been set in place. CSF regulars were on a twelve-hour rotation now. Those not on duty could be found in one of the buildings that served as their barracks. No one had invited us in, so we continued to sleep in and around our deuce. Besides, if we had been assigned to the barracks, they may have noticed that each night four of our men were unaccounted for.

The listening posts had worked well at Gold Base Twelve and I wondered why sarge hadn't "gone public" with the idea. We discussed it amongst ourselves and when we couldn't come up with a decisive answer, we asked him. Sarge explained that the LPs were a good idea, but the CSF had a way of ruining good ideas by making them "standard operating procedure" with a written set of "rules and regulations." None of us could argue with that logic. Even with my limited experience I understood.

We decided to move the listening posts every couple days to avoid the same mistake we had made at GB12. Besides, the tarps we used here were easy to set up and worked anywhere there was sand, making them effective over most of the planet. This meant patrols would have to stay out well after sundown to facilitate the move, but none of us complained. It was a small price to pay to keep our men safe.

We had been at MOE16 for about twenty days when LP2 reported movement. A large group, maybe fifty or more, moving east to west approximately eight clicks out. The other LPs had not seen anything. The next morning sarge rode gunner in my speed-track and we went out to see what we could find. There had definitely been a large group come through. The only good news was the lack of vehicle tracks. Most likely it was just marauders traveling at night to avoid any run ins with other tribes.

Two days later, LP4 had a similar experience. Once again, the group was moving west and appeared to be on foot. There were several possibilities now. Could be just coincidence, two tribes moving in roughly the same direction at roughly the same time. Might be some sort of marauder gathering, we had heard reports of these happening in the past. Worst case, they were on their way to meet up with the Indingos to make an attack on MOE16. Sarge decided to bring the evidence to the base commander. To avoid any mention of our listening posts he played it off as OrP finding tracks in the sand during a routine patrol.

According to the Captain, the evidence was not strong enough to warrant an increase in security measures. Besides, it's not as if he had any additional men to stand duty. Sarge suggested moving the J-tracks with the one-inch blasters into a more prominent position, perhaps up on the rock shelf with the mining equipment. There, they would be slightly elevated and capable of firing over the perimeter fence rather than through it, should the base come under attack. The Captain wasn't about to take advice from an OrP sergeant until sarge pointed out it would better serve to protect the valuable mining equipment which was the entire purpose of our being there. By late afternoon three of the J-tracks were in place on the rock shelf, though they remained unmanned.

By the fortieth day at MOE16 everyone had settled into a routine. The dining hall was fully operational, and men filed in for meals at the appropriate times. Engineers drove their machines, moving materials and helping to get the rest of the buildings assembled. Even the OrP was getting lulled into a sense of security with our daily changing of the LP and repeated patrols of the same old dunes. The gate guards no longer bothered to look at us when we approached, preferring to just let us come and go at will so they could continue their conversations. If you know anything about war, you know this is not a good thing. Complacency gets people killed.

Sarge was on edge and he was taking it out on all of us. Currently the mechanic was enduring a shitstorm of ferocity from him over the fact that the busted down speed-track we had brought along was still inoperable. "You mean to tell me that we drug this wreck all the way out here with all these damn parts and you still can't make it function?" Each word was punctuated with a kick to the fender of the broken-down ST. A river of profanity poured from sarge's mouth as he stomped away, glancing around in hopes of locating another suitable outlet for his anger. All of us looked at our boots to avoid making eye contact with the rampaging man.

That's when the shooting started. The marauders were coming over the dunes to the west. Hundreds of them firing wildly with all kinds of weapons. Blasters and projectile type weapons zinged and boomed accordingly, burning metal and punching holes as we tried to find cover. Four of our speed tracks were on patrol outside the fence and sarge yelled for the mechanic to "grab a radio and recall our men, NOW! Everyone else grab your long-arms, get to the J-tracks, and man those one inchers. Don't let em get through the fence!"

I had expected to see the CSF guys clambering for the J-tracks, but they had seemingly forgotten about them and were taking up defensive positions near the west perimeter, using the heavy equipment for cover and returning fire whenever possible. From the elevated rock shelf we could see them coming over the dunes like water poured from a bucket. I froze at the sight, unsure whether it was best to go the other way or stay and fight until we were overrun. My gunner nudged me then, he was yelling but it sounded like he was in a tunnel miles away. "LET'S GO!" I snapped back, jumping into the driver's seat and starting the J-track. He was already in position, adjusting the guns elevation as I swung the vehicle around to face the onslaught. WUMPF! The big blaster went off with no discernable effect to the ocean of marauders. Now the other two J-tracks were in position and firing. Wumpf, wumpf, wumpf! The sand was exploding now and slowly the tide was being parted a little with each volley.

Eventually we could see the top of the dunes, where before we could only see the mass of rauders. My gunner adjusted the elevation down as low as he dare, being careful that his shots not hit the fence. I glanced towards the fence, curious to see if it was holding. Cloaked bodies were piling up at the base of the fence as others stepped on them in an attempt to climb over the perimeter. Suddenly there was an explosion. One of the CSF regulars must have thrown a MPED. It had struck the fence at about head height before going off. The resulting hole was just what the rauders needed. The sheer press of bodies pushed our attackers through the breech and into the base.

Outside the fence a half-track and three speed-tracks were approaching from the north, shooting into the mass of men. The whole scene was surreal, like a terrible dream with no escape. Once again, my gunner brought me back. "They've found a hole! Swing her a little left!" I swung the machine a bit more left as he brought the barrel down to bear on the opening created by the grenade blast. Wumpf! Wumpf! Wumpf! It was a sickening sight. The one-inch blaster was intended for taking out machinery and structures at a considerable distance. At close range it tore holes in the ranks of men as they tried to push their way through the widening gap in our perimeter. The other two J-tracks saw what was happening and followed suit.

Several marauders had made it inside the fence before we turned the big guns on them and were doing their best to take on the CSF regulars. The rauders were fierce. When their longarms overheated, they would swing them like clubs, bashing away at their enemies with blind rage. Then, just as suddenly as it had begun, it was over. The marauders outside the fence began a tactical retreat. Firing from the hip as they backed away then turning and sprinting over the dunes. Sarge, in the half-track and the three Outriders in their speed-tracks, followed from a safe distance, just to be certain they weren't going to regroup for a second attack.

Once convinced there would be no immediate follow-up, we went to work. The engineers set to repairing the damaged section of fence. CSF soldiers sent two details outside the fence. One group retrieved weapons from the fallen marauders and loaded them into a deuce-track. The second group threw the dead men onto a flatbed. Every so often the trailer full of dead would be hauled a couple clicks to the south and emptied into a mass grave. A second smaller hole was dug for the CSF soldiers who had been killed.

During training we had been told that for a "fair shipping fee" we could have our bodies transported back to our home planet for burial. It was a scam of course. The fine print in the agreement stipulated that "the Colonial Security Force will not be held accountable in the event... due to unforeseeable circumstances... bodies may be disposed of on planet if transport to a shuttle is not readily available." In other words, if you die anywhere besides Supply Base 01, you're getting planted in the sand.

***

Sarge had been on edge before the attack, but

afterwards he was far worse. We had lost two men and a speed-track out there. No sign of them was found, but we were forced to confine the search to no more than four clicks from the base for fear of running in to the marauders and losing more Outriders. Sarge decided to abandon the listening posts until further notice as well. No sooner had he made this announcement than he retired to the cab of our deuce with a bottle. We did not see him again until the following morning.

Four weeks later nearly a hundred more CSF regulars showed up with just over a hundred civilian colonists and miners. MOE16 was not intended to hold so many bodies and plans were made to alleviate some of the pressure. Once again, the heavy equipment was loaded on to the flatbeds and chained down. The engineers and a few deuces full of soldiers were all preparing for the return to SB01. One of the J-tracks along with a couple half-tracks would also be making the trip. Of course, the column had to have forward and flank support in the form of speed-tracks. Who else could possibly "make first contact when necessary in order to give the company time to assume a defensive posture?"

CHAPTER SIX - THE
BEST DEFENSE

The trek back to Suck a Big One was strange. Of the eight days we were on the move, we saw marauders on six different occasions. Each time they were quite some distance from the column and showed no interest in us. At first, we thought perhaps they were shadowing us, then it became apparent it was not a single band but rather several different groups. It was as if they had us surrounded but wanted to avoid us. Even sarge had no idea what to make of their unusual behavior.

Back at SB01 they had a surprise for us. Three new transfers were waiting in the barracks. Outside the barracks armed Patrolmen were making sure the new members remained under house arrest until our return. No doubt the brass knew we had lost two men at MOE16 and were cleaning the miscreants out of some other platoons to fill the void. We were glad to see replacements, but now we had seventeen men and only seven working speed-tracks. This put pressure on our mechanic to get the two busted speed-tracks going. For his part sarge started working on the quartermaster to get the parts needed to make them both field worthy.

For the rest of us, it was back to the old grind.

The new guys went out with the close patrols. We would let them drive most of patrol, then once they were doing well, we'd let them try their hand in the gunner's seat. Driving the speed-tracks isn't difficult, but it does take some practice. We had no idea when we would be going out again, so it was imperative we get these guys trained as soon as possible. The new guys understood what it meant to be assigned as an Outrider and they paid close attention to the training. It was one thing to cause trouble on Indigo Divum, but none of us wanted to die any sooner than necessary.

About three weeks later our mechanic, with sarge's help, managed to get one of the busted speed-tracks back to spec. The remaining ST was too far gone. Anything that could be salvaged from it was removed and saved for future use. Sarge filled out all the necessary forms to have the remains decommissioned but the quartermaster assured him a replacement would probably not arrive for at least a year if it showed up at all. The logic was that Outriders were expendable, why waste money on properly equipping them.

We had a few successes on our records, but they weren't enough to change the general opinion. The brass only needed us to absorb enemy fire, so we continued to be a dumping grounds for undesirable soldiers, men who didn't follow orders, who failed to respect their "superiors." Despite what they thought of us we continued to do the best job we could. Not because we cared about their opinions, but because we didn't want to see soldiers die. That was the real difference between us and the upper echelon, to us, every man's life was important.

*****

The first colony on Indigo Divum was built where Supply Base 01 now stands. The early colonists felt a need to set up other smaller settlements in hopes of finding different soil types better suited to growing crops. They referred to these small settlements as outposts and named them accordingly, Indigo Divum Outpost 01, 02, 03, and so on. During the Indingo revolt Outpost 01 and 02 were destroyed. The revolutionaries took everything of value, food, vehicles, tools, generators, everything. The few colonists who survived did so by fleeing to what would become known as Supply Base 01, though at that time it was called Colonial Base 01. Surprisingly, Outpost 03 is still a functioning colony with a CSF company stationed there for protection from both Indingos and marauders.

Sarge received word that we would be escorting a column headed for Outpost 03. The commander there had discovered a marauder tribe setting up camp within easy striking distance and requested reinforcements. It was only a two-day trip to OP3 but they wanted to leave soon in hopes of getting there before the second oldest base on the planet came under attack, so we scrambled to get our gear loaded into the deuce with some spare parts for the speed-tracks.

Within an hour we were ready to go but the regulars were still getting the rest of the column in order. Two J-tracks were being loaded on to a flatbed while CSF regulars would be riding in personnel carriers and of course there was no end of supplies being sent along by deuce. The plan was for them to work through the night so we could leave just before dawn. We knew they would want the column to keep moving until it arrived at Op3, so we stayed in our barracks all afternoon in an effort to remain rested.

Right before dusk, three CSF Patrolmen entered the barracks with another new transfer. This one was obviously dangerous, and the Patrolmen weren't taking any chances. Our new Outrider was maybe five and half feet tall, 135 pounds, and female. They turned her over to sarge and removed the restraints before cautiously backing out the door. She was nervous and her eyes darted about the barracks as if she might be attacked at any moment.

Sarge brought her up to speed on our current situation, how we would be leaving for Outpost 03 as soon as the rest of the column was ready. He also told her that, to his knowledge, no woman had ever been assigned to the Outriders Platoon. Next, he asked her to explain just how she had come to be in our little band of cannon fodder. As she rubbed her wrists where the restraints had dug in, she glanced around the barracks before her eyes finally locked with sarge's and told us the whole story.

It seems throughout her training a certain

lieutenant had been having his way with her. She had remained silent about it primarily out of shame figuring that once she had finished the training, she wouldn't have to see him again and could forget it had ever happened. Two days after completing her training she was awaiting transfer to a permanent assignment when the lieutenant had followed her into a utility closet. Cornered and unwilling to be a victim yet again she broke a wooden mop handle and shoved the splintered end into his stomach with the strength that only pent up anger mixed with fear can provide. As he lay on the floor screaming obscenities at her she twisted the handle shoving it deeper into the man who had violated her repeatedly in the past. His shrieks of pain had brought people running and what they found was a bloody mess of a man being kicked in the face by a female recruit.

I already knew the answer, but had to ask the man's name, just to be certain. She confirmed my suspicions, it was the same lieutenant I had "assaulted" before joining the Outriders. She relaxed a little once I explained my experiences with him. Someone had told her his injuries were quite severe, lacerated bowel, torn kidney, broken nose and orbital fracture. Personally, I felt as if he had gotten off easy.

Sarge gave her his sidearm and told her to hold on to it. It was too late to get her properly trained and outfitted so she would be in the deuce for this trip. We now had eighteen Outriders but only eight working speed-tracks. For this trip, the deuce would be our mobile barracks. Anyone not out on an ST would be driving the deuce or trying to get some rest in the back of it.

Just as expected, two hours before dawn, we got the call to form up. It was a small column and a short hop to Outpost 03 but of course the brass wanted to keep us moving through the night. A day and a half later we were unloading our gear and looking at the latest satellite images of the area.

The marauder encampment that had caused all the commotion was over thirty clicks to the west of Op3. Sarge decided to limit our patrols to no more than three clicks out. That would be far enough to provide warning in the event of an attack but close enough to prevent losing any more men. He also gave us orders not to engage the marauders under any circumstances. Four STs went out immediately with orders to return promptly at sundown. The remaining four would be going out the following morning.

The next day sarge called the patrols in around midday. Apparently, the commander had decided the best defense was a good offense. Plans were being made for an attack on the marauder's encampment. Our part in this offensive was a matter of extensive discussion. Four of our men would be operating a couple J-tracks since we had used them effectively at MOE16. That would free up two of our speed-tracks for the remaining Outriders, including Sarge and the newest arrival to the platoon.

While the CSF infantry attacked the marauder's camp from the near side, the J-tracks, posted on high dunes to the rear, would be lobbing in blasts to the far side to cut off their escape. The Outriders with speed-tracks would be between the infantry and the J-tracks. Their speed and mobility would allow them to bolster forces where needed should the enemy break through our line.

The remainder of the day was spent getting ready for the attack. Outriders don't require much time to prepare. Typically, we can be ready for just about anything in a matter of minutes, but this was different. This was a full-scale attack on a marauder encampment, something none of us had ever done. Gear was checked and double checked. Weapons were cleaned and oiled. Speed-tracks were scrutinized from every angle, adjustments made and then checked again. The process kept us busy enough that we didn't stop to think about what might happen. Being buried in sand with the rest of the dead was not something we wanted to dwell on. Most of us did not sleep that night.

A few hours before sunrise the attack force formed up outside the gates. Infantry in their personnel carriers, Outriders with speed-tracks, and those damn J-tracks. The J-tracks were slow moving and the entire regiment would be forced to crawl along at their pace. The only good news was they would be stopping nearly five clicks out. The personnel carriers would unload then, and the infantry would continue on foot. Once in position, the infantry would radio coordinates to the J-tracks. When the one-inch blasters found their marks, the ground assault would begin. Our platoon would be hanging back half a click to respond as needed.

To our surprise, everything went pretty much as planned. The big blaster rounds dropped on the west side of the marauders camp and the infantry opened fire on the eastern edge. Sarge had us move our STs on to a dune ridge so he could watch the attack. Even from there it was obvious the battle was very one sided. The marauders were trapped between a wall of infantry and the J-track's explosive blasts. After a few minutes they radioed the J-tracks to adjust their fire and "close the window" a little.

The J-tracks fire a plasma blast, like our long-arms, but with a full one-inch bore. The blasts burn through just about anything, except sand. When the white-hot blasts hit the sand, they turn it to molten glass which splashes outward in all directions. The hot glass burns through clothing and skin alike. From our position on the ridge, we could see the effect it was having on the marauders. The ones who survived the shower of liquid glass ran directly into the infantry fire.

After fifteen minutes, the infantry called for the J-tracks to cease fire so they could advance into the remains of the enemy encampment. They met very little resistance as they made their way from one smoldering tent to another, ending the suffering for the wounded they encountered along the way. While the infantry finished up, the CSF wounded were loaded onto a single Personnel carrier. We would be escorting the J-tracks and the wounded back to Op3 immediately. Once they had completed the "clean up" the infantry would hike back to the personnel carriers and return to Op3 on their own. There would be no burial for the marauders. Not even a mass grave.

Later, we heard the official report. Twelve CSF dead, thirty-six wounded. The body count for the marauders was one hundred and twenty-eight with nearly thirty of those being female. There was no mention of children.

The attack had been a success by nearly any definition of the word. The infantry had quite a celebration that evening. None of us wanted anything to do with the celebration, so we volunteered for gate and sentry duties. Maybe the view from the line was different than what we had seen from the ridge. We had no problem firing directly into the waves of marauders as they attacked MOE16, but this was different somehow. This just didn't feel right.

With the marauder encampment neutralized, sarge made a formal request for us to return to SBO1 so we could "be available to perform our duties to their fullest." The request was approved, and we left the following morning. The remainder of the original column would return on their own the following day.

The minute we arrived back at SBO1, sarge informed us that we were "confined to barracks until further notice." The order did not sit well, but we were all too tired to argue. Hot showers and some rack time were our only real concerns.

We woke up to the smell of coffee. Sarge and the mechanic were bringing in trays of hot food from the garage. Apparently, they had used the deuce to transport several trays from the mess hall along with a large container of fresh coffee. Furthermore, it didn't look like the stuff they typically served to the regs. This stuff all looked fantastic, it must have come from the officer's mess. Nobody even asked how or why, we just grabbed a tray and loaded up. The entire day was spent eating, talking, just relaxing.

Late in the afternoon sarge made a point of reminding us we were still confined to the barracks. A few minutes later he produced a large bottle, poured some in his coffee cup, then handed it off to us. Once again, we didn't ask questions, we just loaded up.

The following day we received new orders. We were to escort several empty flatbeds headed for MOE16. Apparently, the mining operation had been a success. The flatbeds would deliver empty shuttle containers and return with containers full of raw eka-caesium-428. If sarge was right, Indigo Divum was now the largest source of EC428 in the known universe.

CHAPTER SEVEN – RICHES

Eka-caesium-87 has been found on Earth but was exceedingly rare and highly unstable. The largest sample ever discovered had a half-life of approximately twenty-five minutes. EC428 is equally reactive but has a half-life of nearly a century making it an excellent source of energy for everything from electric power plants to interstellar transports. I couldn't help but wonder if they had done geological surveys before colonization began. Did the powers that be suspect Indigo Divum would become a source of the most valuable element ever discovered? Not that any of that mattered to us. All we were concerned with was making the trip without losing any of our people.

The column was going to consist solely of flatbeds, armored transports, half-tracks, and us. The plan was to run a straight line to Mining Operations Emplacement Sixteen. They wanted us to push hard. Long days, short nights. Cut the trip to seven days or less if possible. The logic was simple. The flatbeds would not be heavily loaded and what little cargo they carried was not overly valuable, meaning that security would be taking a back seat to haste.

We left before dawn the following day.

We arrived on the seventh day as ordered, but the trip had been hard on the men and the equipment. Both required some maintenance before they could make the return trip. The base commander informed us it would take three days to empty the shuttle containers and refill them with EC428. He expected us to move out at sunrise on day four regardless and that is exactly what we did.

The flatbeds, heavily loaded with full shuttle containers, moved a bit slower on the return trip. We were a full ten days getting back to SB01. No sooner had we arrived than orders were passed down for us to do it all over again. Two days later we left. This time we had four flatbeds carrying empty containers. We would remain at MOE16 until half of them were filled before returning to SB01, then turn around and do it all over again. Seven days to Mining Operation Emplacement 16, two days there, ten days back to SB01, two days there, repeat, repeat, repeat.

Sometime around our twentieth trip I began to wonder why they didn't just send engineers to build a shuttle landing. It had to be a better than escorting the containers over and over. Even sarge was beginning to grumble about the escort duties and the predictability of our movement. Surely the marauders had watched us and recognized the pattern, which raised another obvious question. Why hadn't they attacked? The whole situation felt strange to me, but I kept my thoughts to myself, discounting it as typical CSF incompetence combined with marauder ignorance.

By my count we had made forty-eight round trips with four full container loads of EC428 returning to Suck a Big One each trip. Each container held nearly two tons of the stuff, meaning we had sent approximately three hundred and seventy tons of raw EC428 back for processing when the mine started to give out. The good news was we would be allowed a four-day rest at each location. Then it became six days, then eight. Eventually we were instructed to escort flatbeds of equipment back to MOE16 to retrieve as much of the base as reasonably possible. The mining operation was being shut down.

The engineers pulled up the mining equipment and took down the buildings. Those, along with the j-tracks were loaded onto flatbeds. When the convoy moved out, the perimeter fence was all that remained of MOE16.

CHAPTER EIGHT - BUSINESS AS USUAL.

When we returned to SB01, it was back to standard patrols. The "new girl" was my gunner now. She wasn't new anymore, but the moniker stuck, and she didn't seem to mind. We were on our regular run one day, maybe five clicks outside the perimeter when we saw a column of marauders a full kilometer away. They were just standing there on a ridge. I brought the speed-track to a halt on a large dune. Through the viewer it was clear they were just standing there, watching us, waiting for something, maybe hoping one lone speed-track would engage them. I was voicing my concerns out loud when I heard my partner gasp. Before I could look to see the cause, everything went dark and I lost consciousness.

When I woke it was dark and my head was pounding. Once my eyes adjusted, I could tell this was a marauder tent. My hands were tied tightly behind my back with a rope leading to my ankles and binding them as well. I glanced around hoping to see new girl, but she was not there. For a brief moment I considered squirming under the edge of the tent and attempting to make my way back to SB01. The futility of this plan quickly became obvious. Even if

I could get out of the ropes, which seemed unlikely, and find the speed-track, I had no idea where I was or which way to go. Left with no real options I closed my eyes and drifted off to sleep.

"I'm going to untie your hands so you can eat. Please don't make me regret it."

Once again, my eyes opened to see the inside of a tent, but this time a cloaked figure stood nearby, clearly visible in the light streaming through the open flap. He held a plate in one hand a cup in the other.

"Well? Can you remain civil long enough to eat?" His faint accent was clearly from Earth, perhaps Germanic. He waited patiently as I again considered my options. Finding them to be few and not at all positive, I gave him a nod.

He set the plate and cup on the ground, being careful not to kick sand onto them, before untying my hands. Once finished, he cautiously stood and backed away three full steps. I rubbed my hands together, attempting to bring the feeling back before reaching for the cup.

"It's coffee but I have a bottle of water if you'd prefer."

I used both hands to lift the warm cup to my lips. It was good and felt amazing as it washed the grit from my parched tongue.

"The eggs are scrambled. In truth, they are powdered but the flavor isn't terrible."

As I reached for the plate covered in what looked like yellow sponge the coffee kicked in,

"Where's my partner?"

"She's here, in another tent, also having breakfast." My face betrayed my doubts as I looked at my captor. "I assure you no harm will come to her at our hands. Despite what you may have heard, we are not animals."

"I want to see her."

"In time. But first you need to eat. When you are feeling better, we'll take a walk. Here, keep this water, you'll probably want it once you finish eating." He placed a metal bottle at my side. "If you want anything else, there's a guard outside who will see to your needs. I'll be back in a little while. Again, please don't make me regret untying you."

"Got any bacon?"

A broad smile crossed his face, "I fear we don't get much bacon out here. Perhaps some more eggs?" Even in the low light of the tent, he could see my head shaking in response, "Alright then. I'll be back soon; we can talk more then."

His voice did not sound menacing at all, but some small part of my brain hinted he intended that as a threat. Perhaps a bit of torture was in my future. No matter, I don't know much anyway. Least ways nothing of use to these guys. I hoped he was telling the truth about the new girl. She would not take well to any rough treatment.

Through the thin walls of the tent could be heard all the usual sounds of a military unit. Men passing along orders, swapping duties for cigarettes, exchanging vulgar jokes, loud laughter, and plenty of foul language. If I closed my eyes, I could easily imagine this was a CSF encampment.

My feet had gone numb, so I untied them. The blood rushing back caused them to throb with pain. Several minutes later, I was able to stand with only slight discomfort. The guard must have heard me moving around. He poked his head in through the door and quite casually asked if I needed anything.

"Got anything good to drink?"

He stepped inside, the longarm slung across his back, bulged under the cloak that seemed to be the uniform of the marauder. He reached to a hip pocket, the motion causing me to freeze momentarily, fearing he was about to swing the longarm in my direction. Instead he produced a battered flask which he opened carefully before taking a quick drink and handing it to me.

"Just a sip. This has to last for a few more days at least."

This couldn't be happening. I must be dreaming. Was I really sharing a drink with a marauder?

It was some true rotgut that burned my throat and ignited my chest as it sucked the oxygen from my lungs. Barely able to breathe I managed a nod and handed the flask back.

"Sorry, I should have warned you. It's pretty rough stuff." He resealed the flask and returned it to its hiding place. "I better get out there. The captain will be back soon."

He was right. A matter of a few minutes and the man who had brought me breakfast returned.

"I see you removed the rest of the restraints. Feel well enough to take a walk?"

"After you, captain."

He grinned slightly at my answer then threw the tent flap open and exited. Outside it was a typical Indigo Divum day. Sunny and beautiful. The captain motioned for me to walk beside him.

"Not what you were expecting, are we?"

"When can I see my partner?"

"Ok. I get it. You think this is a trick. We feed you, treat you decent, then torture you until we get what we want. Is that it?"

"Isn't that the usual M.O.? We are enemies after all."

"That last part remains to be seen." The captain stopped and turned towards me. "Here's the deal. We are not going to torture you or your partner. We don't want any information from either of you. All that I ask is that you listen to what I have to say. If I ask you any questions along the way, they will be for you to answer to yourself, not out loud and certainly not to me. I already have the answers as you will soon see. If that sounds reasonable to you, I will proceed."

"And what if I have questions along the way?"

The caption smiled again. "I'll do my very best to answer them, but you must agree to hear me out. Shall I begin?"

"Alright. I'll listen."

"You came from Earth. Do you remember the CSF screening process? On Earth they took blood and ran a few basic tests to assess your health. Then you were transported to a space station. There you endured further testing performed by seemingly indifferent physicians. The testing went on for days, but the truth is, there was only one test that mattered. The physicians knew the work they did was pointless. If you made it to the space station, you were not going back to Earth. Not ever."

I interrupted him then. "You don't know as much as you think. Plenty of people failed the testing and returned to that burnt out planet."

"Did they? How would you know that? Did you go back with them? Of course not. Now, if I may continue."

The captain paused and waited for me to give him the nod as we once again began to walk through the marauder encampment.

"As I said, days were spent testing your mental stamina, but all they were looking for was a psychiatric profile. You see, everyone has certain traits that make them who they are. Some are quite strict in their lifestyles, preferring to live in a structured environment. Others, artists for instance, tend to thrive on disorganization. Those are the extremes of course. Most people fall somewhere in between. Humanity is a spectrum of various personality types. So, the powers that be created a testing system and divided the spectrum up into fairly predictable workforce groups. Accountants on one end, artists at the other. Somewhere in the middle lies an imaginary line. To the arbitrary left lies the

CSF soldier. To the arbitrary right, the marauder types. Do you understand now?"

"Clear as sand, captain. Keep going."

"Alright. As I said, everyone who gets to the space station gets a job. Some meet the profile of a CSF soldier. Others, like me for instance, fit the profile of the rebel, but everyone gets an assignment based on the test results. The system works reasonably well, but occasionally someone like you comes along who falls just barely to the left of that arbitrary line. Someone who doesn't always care for the structure of the CSF or can't seem to turn a blind eye to the injustices inherent in the system. People like you will invariably end up in the Outriders Platoon. Once we figured it out, we stopped targeting Outriders and chose instead to offer them an opportunity to join us. Does that clear things up for you?"

"Sure does. I see it now. You're nuts."

"And what brought you to that conclusion?"

"You expect me to believe all of us who made it to the space station ended up on Indigo Divum?"

"Of course not. But most of them did. What percentage of the people who were there with you allegedly failed? Something like sixty-five percent, correct? Thirty five percent passed and became CSF soldiers. Another thirty-five percent became marauders. The remaining people were sent to other planets where they could best serve the needs of those in charge."

"Right. Completely logical and believable."

"I'm sensing a bit of sarcasm."

"I hope so, I was spreading it on pretty thick."

"For the moment, let's consider some things you know to be true. How many trips did you make while escorting the EC428 shipments back to SB01? Over fifty, by my reckoning. Did you ever wonder why they didn't just put in a shuttle pad at MOE16? Did you ever wonder why the shipments never came under attack? Fifty round trips between SB01 and MOE16 without a single skirmish. Seems a bit unlikely doesn't it?"

"Do tell, captain. Why? Why no shuttle pad? Why no attacks?"

"We didn't attack because we received orders stating the shipments were not to be interrupted. You see, we take orders from the same people. We get supplied by the same people."

"Sorry, captain, but we don't take orders from the Indingos."

"There are no Indingos. Haven't been for years. The Indingos were just a bunch of idealistic kids. They didn't hurt anyone. They tried to start a little rebellion after the geological surveys revealed the likelihood of eka-caesium. They wanted to create their own utopia by selling the element to Earth. The powers that be couldn't allow that. The CSF was dispatched to put an end to it. Fearing future generations might follow in the Indingos footsteps the Marauders were created to keep the civilians in a state of fear. To keep us supplied and prevent the truth from coming to light a new shuttle landing site was erected on the opposite side of the planet. For further security, no aircraft are allowed on Indigo Divum. The whole thing is rather ingenious and has worked well for over five ID decades."

"Captain, with all due respect, you're full of shit."

"I realize it's a lot to absorb, take a few minutes to process it all."

"For the sake of argument, let's assume you are telling the truth. What happened to the Outriders at MOE16? We lost two during the marauder attack that day."

"I was hoping you would get around to asking that question. One of them is here in camp. He's posted outside your partner's tent."

"And the other?"

"He is alive and well but assigned to another platoon."

"And what about the OrP lieutenant? Is he here or conveniently stationed elsewhere as well?"

"Lieutenant? The one we captured near SB01 a few years ago? You know, we got him the same way we got you, in the same area even. No, he chose a different path."

The captain stopped now. We had walked as we talked and now found ourselves near one of the many crater lakes that dotted the planet.

"I told you earlier that no harm would befall you or your partner at our hands. That, like everything I've told you, is true. When we are fortunate enough to successfully capture an Outrider, we tell them these things, then they are given a choice.

Were you at Gold Base Twelve when we tried to get five Outriders at once? That was a failure on our part. We completely underestimated the OrP."

"Yes, I was there. We didn't lose a single man."

"Wish I could say the same."

"You mentioned a choice?"

"Ah yes. I have this conversation with every Outrider we capture. At the end of the discussion, he is given the option of joining us, becoming a marauder, or…" The captain made a sweeping gesture towards the lake. "Or going for a swim. I can't say for certain it is a quick end, but to date, nobody has complained."

"The lieutenant chose to swim?"

"He was a stubborn man. He refused to see the facts. Refused to believe the truth. In all honesty, I was not surprised."

"You are asking me to choose between my enemy and certain death."

"If you truly feel that way, you have missed the point of our conversation. We all serve the same master. Marauders are as important to the safety and security of this planet as the CSF. Earth is pulling the strings and we all do its bidding. None of us are getting off this planet alive. You can keep fighting or you can quit right here and now." Again, he gestured to the water.

"Just to be certain I understand this correctly, you're telling me that whoever is in power on Earth is supplying this planet with people for the sole purpose of extracting EC428. The war between the CSF and the Marauders is funded entirely by Earth for the purpose of keeping the civilians in line. Is that the gist of it?"

The captain's face became even more sullen. "Yes. That is correct. Perhaps a bit over simplified, but accurate nonetheless."

"And my choices are to keep playing my part in this fiasco or take my own life?"

"Basically. However, I feel it pertinent to point out that it really isn't much different than the choices you had on Earth. There you were simply ignorant of the role you played. Here, now, you know the truth of your situation."

It was a lot to take in. While it all sounded ridiculous, it also answered several questions. Why didn't we have any air support here? Why didn't the CSF just take out the Indingos entirely? Why did we have satellite imaging but still no idea where the Indingos were? If the captain was crazy, he was also a genius. The other option was that he was simply honest. What was that thing I read about back on Earth? Something about the simple answer being most likely.

"Well captain, I guess in the back of my mind, I always knew there was no getting off this planet. To be honest, why would anyone want to leave? It's beautiful here. Far better than Earth. To hell with the CSF, where do I get one of them cloaks?"

The Captain's eye's gleamed as a broad smile creased his face. "Excellent. I'll get you one personally, but first we must speak to your partner."

GLOSSARY

Colonial Security Force or CSF, a military organization created for the sole purpose of protecting Earth's assets on colonized planets.

Deuce-track, a military truck used in difficult terrain. These vehicles have front wheels but utilize tank style treads in place of rear wheels. The deuce-track is used as the modern-day mule, carrying soldiers, gear, and supplies.

EC428, eka-caesium-428, an extremely rare and reactive element commonly considered to be the most valuable isotope known to man.

Half-track, the preferred vehicle of officers on Indigo Divum, it carries no weaponry and serves as little more than a status symbol. Roughly twice the size of a speed-track, it can carry up to four people and like most vehicles on ID it has tracks in place of rear wheels.

Indigo Divum or ID, a habitable planet at the far reaches of the Earth's colonization efforts, it is predominantly sand with crater lakes scattered across the surface. Indigo Divum has an oxygen rich atmosphere and early geological surveys suggest it may be rich in rare elements as well.

Indingos, the self-proclaimed indigenous peoples of Indigo Divum, they were the first generation of people to be born on the planet.

J-track, basically a self-propelled canon with a one inch bore firing plasma blasts intended to cut through structures and vehicles up to ten kilometers away.

Listening Post or LP, a one- or two-man position stationed away from the main force. The purpose of the LP is to detect enemy movement and provide warning of a possible attack.

Longarm, a small caliber plasma weapon fired from the shoulder.

M.O., modus operandi, the standard method of doing something.

Marauders or rauders, are warring nomads who wander across the surface of Indigo Divum, attacking settlements, mining operation and even rival tribes.

MPED, manually propelled explosive device available in several different types with the following three being most prevalent. Hex (hexachloroethane) produces copious amounts of dense white smoke. P-15 (phosphorous) showers the area with white hot burning metal. Pb-82 (lead ball) detonation sends hundreds of lead balls flying in every direction.

Outrider Platoon or OrP, a unit of the Colonial Security Forces whose purpose is to serve as flank guards for bases, mining operations, and military convoys.

Outrider, any member of the Outrider Platoon.

Spec, slang for specification. Meeting the

minimum requirements of safe operation.

Speed-track or ST, these machines are just large enough to carry to men and a minimum of gear. The speed-track is reserved for use by Outriders as it is capable of moving swiftly into battle. As the name implies, the ST is driven by treads, like nearly all other military vehicles on Indigo Divum. It is armed with a .30 caliber plasma blaster that can be operated by the driver or from the gunner's seat.

Stimtabs, the military prescribed amphetamine-based stimulant used sparingly by soldiers who must stay alert for long periods of time.

ABOUT GUY

I can't remember a time when I wasn't enjoying the outdoors. As a child my father taught me to hunt and fish. Later, in the Boy Scouts, I found that the nature merit badges were my favorites to earn on my trail to Eagle Scout. Years after, it occurred to me that the things I had learned in my youth were not common knowledge. In fact, many simply had no clue how to behave in the outdoors, let alone survive in it. Ultimately, I founded Zombie Apocalypse Survival Camp to help families learn together so they can perform as a cohesive unit in the event of a catastrophe.

Somewhere along the way I tried my hand at writing articles on some of the less obvious aspects of survival, like possible apocalypse currencies, using brush piles for survival, and more. A few of these have been published in Backwoodsmen Magazine.

Whether it's hunting, fishing, camping or just a nice long hike with my dogs, for me, being outdoors is the remedy to all life's problems.

Read more great stories from Guy Cain, available at Amazon.com!